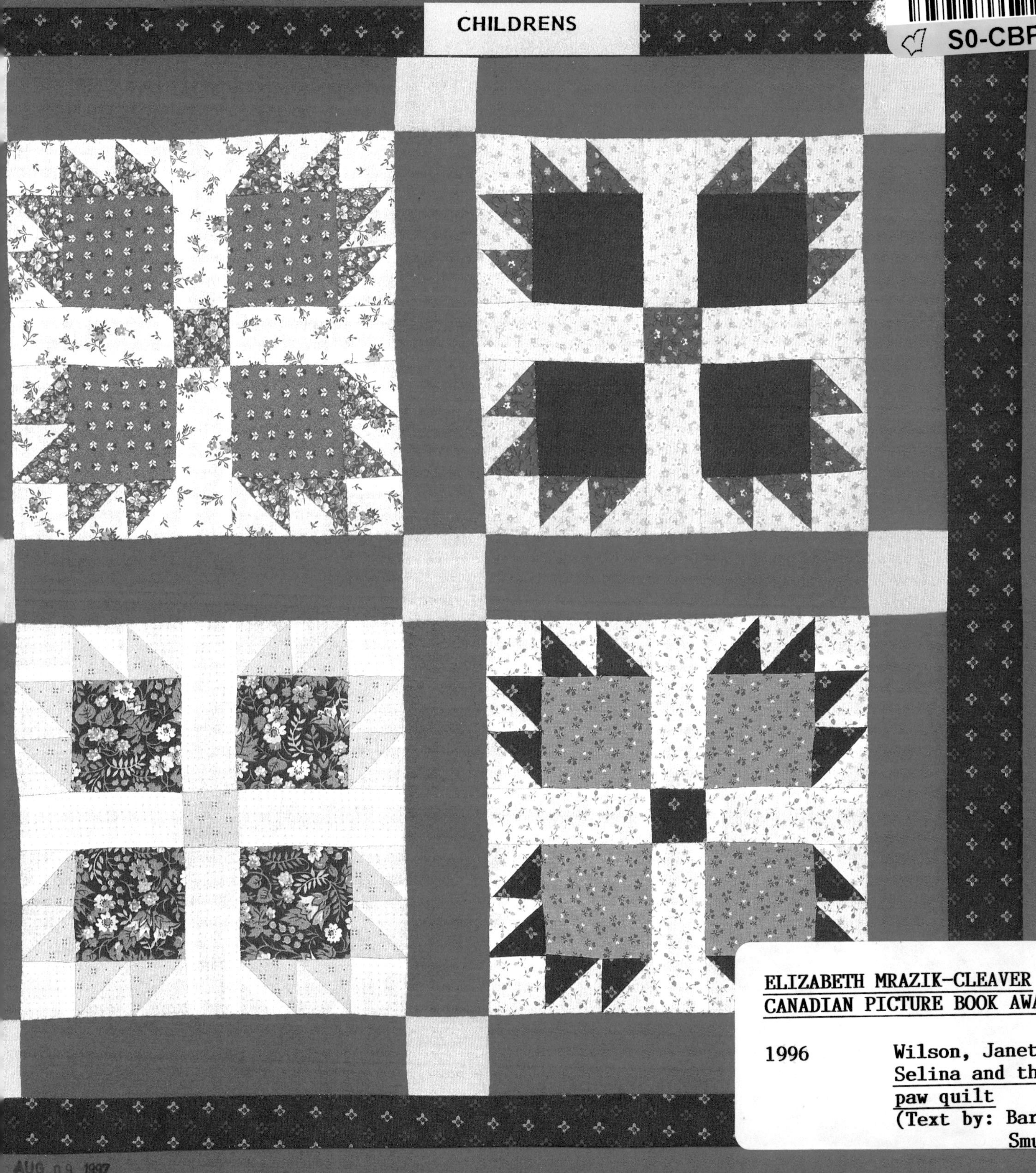

SELINA AND THE BEAR PAW QUILT

BARBARA SMUCKER

Illustrated by JANET WILSON

LESTER PUBLISHING

*To Lorna Shantz Bergey of Kitchener, Ontario, who owns the Bear Paw
quilt upon which this fictional story is based and whose grandfather migrated
from Pennsylvania to Waterloo, Ontario, during the Civil War.*

— B. S.

For my mother, Dorothy Reid, with love.

— J. W.

Text copyright © 1995 by Barbara Smucker
Illustrations copyright © 1995 by Janet Wilson

Lester Publishing Limited acknowledges the financial assistance of the Canada Council,
the Ontario Arts Council, and the Ontario Publishing Centre.

Canadian Cataloguing in Publication Data

Smucker, Barbara, 1915–
    Selina and the bear paw quilt

ISBN 1-895555-70-1

I. Wilson, Janet, 1952–   II. Title.

PS8537.M83S4   1995   jC813'.54   C95-930773-7
PZ7.S58Se   1995

Lester Publishing Limited
56 The Esplanade
Toronto, Ontario
Canada M5E 1A7

Printed and bound in Hong Kong

95 96 97 98 5 4 3 2 1

INTRODUCTION

The Civil War will rank forever as both the darkest and the most heroic period in American history. It was a conflict that pitted brother against brother, neighbor against neighbor, friend against friend. Sleepy little towns that had once been home to only a few thousand people became living symbols of strife and hatred, strength and courage. Their names were Shiloh, Cold Harbor, Gettysburg.

Emotions ran so high it was almost impossible not to choose sides. But at least one group tried to stay out of the conflict. They were the Mennonites. Throughout their history, these people, who have always lived simply and held strongly to their beliefs, tried to avoid war and bloodshed. They would never take up arms — especially not against their fellow countrymen. Violence was — and is — contrary to the teachings of their church.

Because the Mennonites would support neither the North nor the South, they were considered disloyal by both. They were persecuted, their lands ruined, and some of their meeting places destroyed. Ironically, most Mennonites had come to America from Europe to escape exactly the kind of hostility and unrest they now saw being played out on their doorsteps. They had hoped to find tolerance and acceptance and freedom. Instead, many decided they had no choice but to flee again, and so they headed north to what was then called Upper Canada and is now Ontario.

As was the case with many Mennonites, the family in this story is driven apart by the war. But they soon discover that the ties between them can bridge even the great distances that separate them. For the United States as a whole, also in danger of being divided forever by this costly battle, the greatest victory came with the realization that the bonds holding it together were far more enduring than the forces threatening to tear it apart.

Selina took a deep breath. The spring air smelled of the wheat and barley growing in the fields. "Grandma," she cried, hugging herself, "the meadow looks like a quilt of flowers."

Grandmother smiled as she rocked in her sunny corner. Her thimble, needle, and thread flashed as she pieced together small bits of cloth.

Reluctantly, Selina lowered her head and stared at the mound of bread dough on the flour-covered table beneath the window.

"Selina, you must learn to make your fingers work as fast as your tongue," scolded Mother. "We need the rest of that dough ready for baking soon. Tomorrow there will be aunts and sisters and cousins here for a quilting bee to finish Grandmother's Friendship Star quilt, and your father will be coming home from his visit with Uncle Jacob in Virginia."

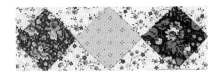

"I can't wait for tomorrow!" Selina clapped her hands together, scattering flour all over both herself and the scrubbed and polished kitchen floor.

Mother shook her head, but when she looked at Selina, there was tenderness in her dark eyes. "When will you learn to be humble and quiet?" she sighed.

Now Selina paid attention to her work. She kneaded every scrap of dough, patted it gently into the pans, and set the loaves aside to rise. Mother would decide when it was time to put them into the hot oven.

Selina washed her hands and went to stand by her grandmother's side. She reached for her own sewing basket on the wooden dish dresser nearby. "What is the pattern for your new quilt?" she asked.

"It's called a Bear Paw quilt," Grandmother whispered, as though it might be a secret. "I got the pattern from a British lady in Lancaster, and I bought a new bolt of cloth for it while I was in the city. I'm mixing that with pieces from my scrap bag." She pulled out a smooth dark green fabric from the overflowing bag. "This cloth is from the dress I wore when I married your grandfather Moses." She touched it gently and laid it on the table. Grandfather had died before Selina was born.

Then Grandmother showed her a white cloth sprinkled with daisies. "This is from a set of baby clothes I made for you, Selina, when you were only two. And this yellow is from my dear sister's favorite dress."

Selina touched the treasured pieces gently with her fingertips. "It's as though we've brought the spring flowers in from the fields," she said dreamily, "and put them together in your quilt."

That evening, when the oil lamps were lit, Selina crept to the head of the stairs and watched her mother set up the quilting frame. Spread out on it was the Friendship Star quilt top, with a layer of wool batting inside and a strong cloth underneath.

Selina wanted to be one of the quilters, but Mother had told her she needed more practice. "Work on your stitches on the dishcloth first," she had instructed.

Quilting bees were like holidays for everyone. While the children played outdoors, the women sat around the quilting frame, laughing and chatting. They sewed the three layers of the quilt together with tiny stitches in a pattern that had been traced lightly on the cover.

At the end of the day, everyone gathered to admire the Friendship Star quilt, with its long, thick patches of color.

Night came, and Selina crawled into her bed in her small room upstairs. "What a lovely day. Now if only Father would come home," she murmured to herself. She was almost asleep when she finally heard his horse and buggy coming up the lane. She could just make out the sound of Mother lifting the door latch and hurrying out to meet him.

Father's deep voice drifted through Selina's open window. He spoke firmly to Mother. "We must move to Upper Canada within the month, Annie. War is coming. Soldiers are killing each other by the thousands." He paused to take a deep breath. "Uncle Jacob told me that in Virginia the armies of the South are already saying our people are disloyal. Mennonite property and farmlands are being destroyed. Many of our meeting houses have been burned to the ground."

Mother's sobs shook Selina to the core. Father continued talking in a softer voice. "We can go to Upper Canada. There is work for me at the sawmill of Jacob Snyder. I can save money to buy farmland. It is rich and fertile . . ."

Selina tried to listen further, but soon fell into a troubled sleep filled with dreams of fighting and gunfire.

In the morning Selina raced downstairs and into her father's arms. He still wore his charcoal Sunday suit with the turned-up collar. His eyes were tired, as though he had not slept.

"Is it true, Father," Selina asked, "that we will have to leave our farm? Is war coming?"

"Yes, it is true that we will have to move," he answered wearily. "There is no place for us in a country that is at war. But there will be many relatives and friends for you, Selina, in Upper Canada."

Days of hurried packing followed. There was talk about the train they would ride, with its smoking, wood-burning locomotive.

On some days the excitement bubbled inside Selina when she thought of chugging across the distant land on iron rails. But at other times she was almost overwhelmed with sadness, for Grandmother would be staying behind.

"Selina, I will not go along with you to Upper Canada," Grandmother had explained. "I am old now, too old to start my life again. I'll stay here in Pennsylvania with my brother Noah and his family."

On the day before they were to leave, Grandmother called Selina into the kitchen. "Come, child," she said. "Let's spread out the new quilt top. It's almost finished."

Before them unfolded the warm, bright beauty of the matching pieces of cloth that held memories for everyone in their family.

"I am giving this quilt top to you, Selina. Take it to your new home, and when it is quilted, spread it out over your bed. You will think of me whenever you look at it."

Selina hugged the precious gift tightly in her arms.

A large farm wagon with a four-horse team came the next day to carry Selina and her family to the train station in Lancaster.

There was the locomotive, hissing with steam. Soon the train was rolling through the countryside. The next afternoon the train came to the suspension bridge that crossed the Niagara River into Upper Canada. Thin webs of iron swung perilously through the sky, connecting one country with another. Far down in the gorge, the river churned in rushing whirlpools.

It seemed an eternity before the train finally stopped in Berlin, near Waterloo, where Selina and her family would live. Through the window Selina saw a horse-drawn farm wagon just like the ones at home.

"It's Uncle Isaac Eby!" Father cried, jumping up to greet him.

Uncle Isaac, in his homespun farm clothes, laughed and shook their hands. "You will stay with us until your new house is ready," he said as he led them away.

Aunt Minerva met them at the door, her hands folded over a starched white apron and her smooth brown hair tucked neatly under her head covering. She bent down to take Selina's quilt top from her arms.

"Oh, no." Selina drew back. "It's my quilt top from Grandmother."

"Quilt top!" The four Eby daughters suddenly appeared at the open front door. "Let's spread it out on top of the kitchen table."

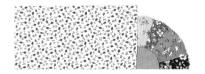

The dark green patches from Grandmother's wedding dress and the flowered daisies from Selina's baby clothes and the many, many squares of memory shone strong and beautiful in the sunny kitchen.

"It's the Bear Paw pattern," Selina told them, thinking of Grandmother as she traced the pattern with her fingertips.

"In Canada we call this pattern Duck's Foot in the Mud," one of her cousins said, laughing. "It came to us here from our English neighbors."

"We'll have a quilting bee soon for Selina's quilt top," Aunt Minerva announced. "And we can order a bolt of flowered red cambric for the backing."

Selina smiled. "I would like the quilt for my bed in our new house when it is finished."

"Of course," everyone agreed.